The Joker

Written by Bill Condon
Illustrated by Craig Smith

™
sundance
A Haights Cross Communications Company

Published by
Sundance Publishing
One Beeman Road
P.O. Box 740
Northborough, MA 01532-0740
800-343-8204
www.sundancepub.com

Copyright © text Bill Condon
Copyright © illustrations Craig Smith

First published 2002 by
Pearson Education Australia Pty. Limited
95 Coventry Street
South Melbourne 3205 Australia
Exclusive United States Distribution: Sundance Publishing

ISBN 0-7608-6742-9

Contents

Characters

Tony is an average sort of guy who likes to play tricks.

Suzanne has plenty of new ideas.

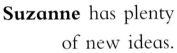

Cory is Tony's best friend. He enjoys a good joke.

David likes to be with his friends.

Chapter One

No More Mr. Average

There wasn't anything unusual about Tony. He wasn't tall, he wasn't fat, he wasn't short, and he wasn't thin. Tony liked to play baseball and soccer with his friends, but he was only an average player. He tried his best at school, but he was only an average student.

"I'm Mr. Average," Tony said to himself. "And I don't like it. I wish I could stand out from the crowd somehow."

It didn't seem that Tony's wish would come true. Then one rainy Sunday something happened that would change his life. Tony was bored. His parents were in the living room, talking with his mom's boss, Mr. Bening. She was serving coffee as Tony walked into the room.

"Tony, can you go to the kitchen and get me the sugar bowl, please?" his mother asked him.

"Sure," Tony said, and he headed to the kitchen. Then he got an idea after noticing the salt shaker next to the sugar bowl. He quickly poured the sugar out of the bowl and replaced it with salt.

Tony handed Mr. Bening the sugar bowl, and his mom's boss used two big spoonfuls. "I have a sweet tooth," he told Tony.

Tony smiled at Mr. Bening and waited while he took a large sip. For a moment, Mr. Bening kept smiling at Tony. Then his face changed, and he began to gag and cough.

"Is everything okay?" asked Tony's mother in a concerned voice. She could see he didn't like his coffee.

Mr. Bening stared at Tony, then took the sugar bowl and tasted what was inside. "It's salt!" he exclaimed. "No wonder the coffee tastes terrible!"

Tony's mom suddenly realized what Tony had done. She looked angrily at her son and reached out to take the sugar bowl from Mr. Bening. "I'm terribly sorry," she said to him, glaring at Tony.

But Mr. Bening, who had been frowning, gave a huge laugh.

"Very good, Tony. That was quite a joke! I thought it was the coffee, and I didn't want to hurt your mother's feelings. But then I remembered I had already taken a sip before you brought the sugar in. I mean, the salt!" Mr. Bening laughed again, even louder. "You have an interesting sense of humor, Tony."

"I have?" Tony was surprised.

"Absolutely," said Mr. Bening. "The world needs more jokers."

After Mr. Bening left, his mom looked at Tony and said, "You know, Tony, not everyone feels the way Mr. Bening does about jokers. A lot of people would have been angry at you for doing what you did. I just want you to realize that."

"Sure, Mom, but he thought I was funny!" Tony replied.

"Well," his dad said, "just remember that jokes aren't fun if they go too far."

"Okay, Dad," Tony replied.

But he was only half listening. He was too busy being pleased with himself. At last he'd found something that he could be good at. From now on, he was going to be a joker!

Chapter Two

Making Trouble

The next day Tony went to Neville's Novelty Shop. He put all of his pocket money on the counter.

"What will this buy?" he asked. Minutes later Tony had bought several rubber snakes and spiders, whoopee cushions, a glow-in-the-dark eyeball, and fake blood capsules. The next day he arrived at school early and put a whoopee cushion on Natasha Peterson's chair.

Tony knew that he needed to distract Natasha before she sat down. Otherwise she'd see the whoopee cushion, and the joke would be ruined. So he put two chocolates on her desk, with a note that said: *From Your Secret Admirer.*

Soon all of the kids walked into class. Natasha saw the chocolates and grinned. "Wow!" she exclaimed happily when she read the note.

Mr. Philips, the teacher, lowered his glasses and peered at Natasha. "Please sit down now," he said sternly.

Tony was so excited he could hardly breathe. He watched as Natasha sat on the whoopee cushion. It made a loud slurpy sound that echoed around the classroom.

Everyone roared with laughter. Natasha squealed, jumped up, and her face turned bright red.

Mr. Philips marched over to her desk, looking angry. But the kids couldn't stop laughing and giggling.

Mr. Philips picked up the whoopee cushion. He dangled it in the air as if it were a dead rat.

"Who brought this to school?" Mr. Philips barked, narrowing his eyes and peering around the classroom.

Ever so slowly Tony raised his hand. "It was me," he admitted. "It was only supposed to be a joke."

"Well, I didn't think it was very funny," muttered Natasha.

"Jokes are fine," said Mr. Philips. "But not in class. Is that clear?"

"Yes," said Tony.

Several of the kids were still smiling. Natasha still looked annoyed.

I won't do any more jokes in class, Tony thought to himself. But no one said anything about outside class. I can hardly wait until recess! I need to plan the next fantastic joke by Tony, king of the jokers!

Chapter Three

The Happy Joker

At recess, Tony dragged his friends David, Cory, and Suzanne over to a shady tree. He started looking up into the tree.

"What's going on?" asked David.

"There's a brand-new baseball up there." Tony pointed up at the branches. "How can we get it down?"

"I'll get it," said Cory.

"I'm taller than you are," said Suzanne. "I'll get it."

"No, I'll get it!" declared David.

Tony stood back as they jumped up and shook the tree's branches. He covered his mouth to stop himself from giggling. Suddenly something fell to the lower branches of the tree. It wasn't a baseball.

"It's a snake!" yelled Suzanne, as a green and orange snake slid from the tree.

"Aarrgghh!" screamed David and Cory.

Laughing hysterically, Tony picked up the snake and wiggled it in front of them. "It's a rubber snake!" Tony cried. "You were scared by a piece of rubber. That is so funny!"

David, Suzanne, and Cory were not impressed. Cory was very annoyed and said dryly, "Ha–ha–ha."

Suzanne sighed, "Grow up, Tony."

"Not funny," added David, and he started to walk away with Cory and Suzanne.

"Wait," said Tony. "I'm sorry." He put out his hand to Suzanne. "Let's shake hands and be friends."

Suzanne thought it over for a moment. "Oh, all right," she said. She stretched her arm toward Tony, reaching for his hand to shake it.

It was a bad idea! In
Tony's hand was an
enormous, hairy
rubber spider.

"Ahhh!" cried
Suzanne at the top
of her voice. She
hated spiders even
more than snakes.

A kid walking by heard her scream and
came over to see what was going on. Tony
decided to have some fun. He threw the
spider at him. It landed on the kid's shoulder.
When the kid saw what it was, he yelped in
fright and smacked the spider off. Then he
ran off. Tony started to laugh, and everyone
laughed with him, including Suzanne.

It was the funniest thing that had ever
happened at recess. Tony was now truly
the king of jokers!

From then on, nothing could stop Tony. His jokes kept getting bigger and better. Before long he'd played jokes on nearly his entire class. A lot of kids agreed he was the best. But one of the kids who disagreed with that was Roger Walker.

"Your jokes are lame," said Roger. "They're old, and they're corny."

"They are not," Tony replied. "I'm the best practical joker in the country."

Roger smirked. "If you're so good, let's see you trick Ms. Armstrong."

All eyes turned to Tony. The kids waited to see if he would try to wriggle out of the challenge. But he knew that he couldn't back down. "No problem," he replied. "It'll be easy."

Tony knew that really wasn't true. Ms. Armstrong was the school principal. She wasn't known for her sense of humor. In fact, no one had ever seen her smile. He wondered how he could possibly play a joke on the principal.

By the time he arrived at school the next day, though, Tony had a plan. He hung around the principal's office until he saw her leave. Quickly ducking inside the office, he left a note on her desk.

In his neatest printing, Tony had written *Please Call Miss Take at 555-7789*. After leaving the note, Tony ran back to his classmates and told them to follow him.

By the time Ms. Armstrong returned to her office, a large group of kids had gathered beneath her open window. She noticed the note on her desk and immediately dialed the number.

"Hello," said Ms. Armstrong crisply. "I am looking for a Miss Take."

"Wait for it!" whispered Tony.

"What do you mean I've made a mistake?" squawked Ms. Armstrong. "I have a message right here, and it says to call Miss . . . " Ms. Armstrong suddenly stopped talking. Then she said, "Never mind," and hung up the phone.

There was a long, long pause, and then the kids heard a strange sound coming from Ms. Armstrong's office. The principal was laughing! All of the kids ran off as fast as they could to share the news with the rest of the school. "You're really a legend now!" they told Tony.

Chapter Four

Out of Control

Tony's reputation as a joker was established. No one was funnier than he was. No one was as clever at pulling off fantastic jokes. But the problem was that Tony didn't know when to stop.

Life became one big joke to Tony. Kids were scared to go anywhere near him. They were afraid that rubber snakes or spiders would leap out at them. Tony was out of control.

One day Suzanne, David, and Cory got together after school. They wanted to discuss what to do about their friend, the joker.

"It was funny for a while," said Suzanne. "But he's really gone way too far now."

Cory agreed. "He came over to my house one night wearing a monster mask," he said. "My mom almost fainted when she opened the door and he jumped up at her."

"We have to stop him," said David. "But how?"

Suzanne suggested that they give Tony a dose of his own medicine and play a practical joke on him. "And I think I know the perfect way to do it!" she added.

They soon had a plan worked out. They'd invite Tony to go with them on a camping trip that weekend—a trip he'd never forget.

"I'd love to go," said Tony when they asked him the next day. And thinking about the tricks he could play, he rubbed his hands together excitedly. "It'll be so cool."

That weekend the four friends set off for the campground next to Dark Swamp. Suzanne's father, Mr. Evans, drove them there on Saturday afternoon.

"You kids can camp over there near the swamp, while I camp here next to the truck," he said. "But you all need to be really careful and stay in the camping area. Don't go wandering off."

"It's not dangerous, is it?" asked Tony.

Mr. Evans rubbed his chin thoughtfully. "Everything should be fine," he said. "It's just that . . ."

"Just what?" asked Tony.

Mr. Evans shrugged. "Just stories I've heard. There's probably nothing to them."

"You mean the ones about the Swamp Creature?" asked David.

"I've heard of it," said Cory. "That monster isn't really around here, is it?"

Tony chuckled nervously. "Swamp Creature? You're kidding, right? There's no Swamp Creature, right Mr. Evans?"

"You kids just stay where I told you, and you'll be fine," answered Mr. Evans. "I'll see you later. Just be careful."

"Okay," Tony said shakily.

Mr. Evans turned and walked back to his truck. "Go ahead and set up your tents. You'll be okay," he said. But he didn't sound too sure.

"Swamp Creature," muttered Tony, as he picked up his camping gear and stomped off to the campsite. "What a laugh."

But then Tony noticed that David, Suzanne, and Cory had never looked so serious. He tried to tell himself that there was nothing to worry about.

Chapter Five

At the Camp

"Let's get the tents set up quickly,"
David said.

Tony rolled his eyes. "Oh, come on!
You don't really believe that stuff about the
Swamp Creature, do you?"

"I'm not sure," David replied. "I've
heard a lot of stories about that creature."

"People make them up—just like ghost
stories," snapped Tony. "I'm sure the
creature is only an imaginary one."

"I don't think so." Cory shook his head. "I saw a news report about this monster on a TV show."

Tony didn't answer. He was too busy staring into the swamp. Then his eyes bulged, and his mouth hung open.

"What is it?" asked Suzanne.

"The cr-cr-cr-creature!" stuttered Tony. "It's the Swamp Creature! Run!"

And Tony ran! The others never even looked at the swamp. They just ran right beside him, their hearts pounding in terror. Tony suddenly stopped and fell to the ground, laughing.

"Gotcha!" he laughed. "You fell for the oldest trick in the book! Boy, oh boy! You all looked so scared!"

David, Suzanne, and Cory trudged back to the campsite in silence. None of them looked happy.

Later they sat around eating sandwiches and telling scary stories. David was in the middle of telling a tale about Big Foot. He stopped when he noticed something unusual and ugly on his plate.

"Oh, yuck!" he said, pushing the food away. "I can't eat this with insects all over my plate!"

On David's plate were several plastic cockroaches. They looked very real in the lamplight.

Tony grinned. "You're all so easy to trick. It's not even a challenge. I get you every time."

"Don't you ever get tired of it?" David asked unhappily.

"Never!" said Tony. "It's way too much fun tricking people."

"For you, maybe," responded David.

Suzanne was telling a story about Count Dracula. Right at the most exciting part, Tony pressed a blood capsule to his neck. Then he collapsed as the fake blood gushed out, crying, "He got me! Count Dracula's got me!"

The others rolled their eyes and exchanged glances. Tony's time would come—soon!

Cory decided not to tell a story. There was no point. Tony would just make a joke of it. He stood up. "Well, I'm going to get some sleep. Good night."

Soon all of the kids were settled in their sleeping bags. It was very quiet outside—but not for long.

Tony started to moan like a ghost. "Oowooohhh! Oowooohhh!" he cried out.

"Oh, go to sleep!" hissed Cory.

But it took Tony a long time to decide to go to sleep. He moaned and groaned while the others ignored him, waiting patiently for him to fall asleep.

When at last the other boys heard Tony snore, they left their tent to tell Suzanne it was time. Suzanne got up, went outside, and blinked her flashlight on and off. It was the signal that the real fun was about to start.

Chapter Six

Swamp Creature!

Tony was awakened by a roaring noise. "Hey, guys," he said. "Did you hear that?"

David lifted his head slowly. "What did you wake me up for? I was having a really great dream."

Suzanne yelled from her tent, "Please, Tony. No more of your dumb jokes."

Tony crawled out of his tent. "It wasn't a joke," he said firmly. "I heard a huge roar! It was just outside the tent. Honest!"

Suzanne yawned and said, "Uh-huh. Sure, Tony." Then she closed her eyes.

Cory and David snuggled back down into their sleeping bags. Tony went from one to the other, shaking them.

"Go back to sleep," they snarled.

"I can't sleep," said Tony nervously. "Not when something's roaming around out there."

"Maybe it was your imagination," suggested David.

"I heard it!" insisted Tony.

"It could have been a cow," said Suzanne sleepily from her tent.

Tony snapped his fingers. "Yes! That's it! It was probably a cow."

"But there's only one way to find out for sure," Suzanne added. "Go and look."

The three kids all closed their eyes and pretended to go to sleep.

Cory snored loudly. Tony thought for a moment, trying to decide what to do. "I will take a look," said Tony. "I'm not scared of some noisy, silly old cow."

Boldly he went out of the tent—and walked straight into the outstretched arms of the Swamp Creature. Tony's mouth dropped open.

It looked like a wild, hairy gorilla! And it was huge! It towered above Tony, beating its chest and growling. Tony's scream could be heard in the next state. David, Cory, and Suzanne quickly came out of their tents.

"Ggggg—ape!" spluttered Tony in terror. "Help me!"

But Suzanne wasn't frightened. She started walking over to the gorilla.

The gorilla growled angrily and moved toward Tony. Tony's face was as white as a sheet.

Suzanne went up to the gorilla and touched its back. The gorilla turned its head and looked at her.

"What are you *doing!* Run, Suzanne!" But Suzanne took no notice of Tony. She smiled instead and said, "Hi, Daddy."

Then she removed the gorilla's head to reveal her father. Mr. Evans smiled at Tony.

"Huh?" blurted Tony.

"Gotcha!" said David.

"Boy, oh, boy!" grinned Cory. "You were so easy to trick!"

"My dad owns a costume store," explained Suzanne. "It was a good trick. Don't you think so, Tony?"

Mr. Evans put his hairy gorilla arm around Tony. "Hope I didn't scare you too much," he said.

"Well," said Tony, "no, not at all."

The others laughed. They had seen the look of terror on Tony's face. But Tony quickly recovered from his meeting with the monster. He began to see how silly he'd been with his jokes. He even laughed with the others about it as Mr. Evans drove them home that night.

"We only did it for your own good," said David.

"Yeah, Tony. You were turning into a practical-joking monster," added Cory.

Tony nodded. "I know," he said, not looking at his friends. "You really taught me a lesson."

"Will you still play practical jokes?" asked Suzanne.

Tony stared out the window. "Well, maybe not as many," he said thoughtfully. "And only jokes that make everybody laugh—like this." Then he turned to face the others, smiling broadly. Stuck to his forehead was a glow-in-the-dark eyeball.